ANIMAL
RESCUE CENTER

The Abandoned Hamster

ANIMAL MAGIC

Other titles in the series:

ANIMAL
RESCUE CENTER

The
Abandoned
Hamster

by TINA NOLAN

tiger tales

This series is for my riding friend Shelley,
who cares about all animals.

tiger tales
5 River Road, Suite 128, Wilton, CT 06897
Published in the United States 2018
Originally published in Great Britain 2007
by the Little Tiger Group
Text copyright © 2007, 2017 Jenny Oldfield
Interior illustrations copyright © 2017 Artful Doodlers
Cover illustration copyright © 2017 Anna Chernyshova
Images courtesy of www.shutterstock.com
ISBN-13: 978-1-68010-419-6
ISBN-10: 1-68010-419-5
Printed in China
STP/1800/0148/0817
All rights reserved
10 9 8 7 6 5 4 3 2 1

For more insight and activities, visit us at www.tigertalesbooks.com

Contents

ANIMAL MAGIC
RESCUE CENTER

🏠 HOME

💗 ADOPT

✋ FRIENDS

MEET THE ANIMALS IN NEED OF A HOME!

HAMLET

Dumped in a garbage can, Hamlet is silky and soft with a sweet face, and he's very friendly! Can you resist?

FRANKIE

Shy but inquisitive, this young ferret's owner has moved away, so he needs a new home. Please help!

BUSTER

Only 3 months old, Buster is friendly and energetic. Come and see— he could be the dog for you!

 NEWS

 HELP US

CONTACT

 DONATE!

HUGO

Sweet Hugo was found in a box on our doorstep. Can you give him a home with lots of cuddles?

PRINCESS, PEARL, AND PETE

Three orphaned kittens with attitude! These lively bundles are purr-fect!

HONEY AND HAPPY

Nosy but irresistible, this brother and sister need a home together—with a good supply of parsley!

Chapter One
Working Magic!

"Okay, Ella, you can take Blossom off the website!" Caleb and Ella Harrison were busy updating the Animal Magic website.

Ella brought the picture of Blossom, the black-and-white stray cat, up on the screen. "Cool!" she said as she pressed delete. Blossom's photo and details vanished.

"She went to live with Emma Matthews on Three Oaks Road,"

Caleb reported. "And the couple from Lakewood came in and took Cleo the spaniel earlier this morning, so she's gone, too, plus we've had two phone calls about Hugo the rabbit, and there's a man who's interested in our beautiful Labrador, Val—"

"Stop!" Ella cried. "I can't keep up!"

It was Saturday morning, and Animal Magic was full to bursting with people eager to adopt pets. Early summer sunshine flooded through the open windows. In the stable across the yard, Mickey the noisy donkey let everyone know he was there.

"Okay, I've taken Blossom and Cleo off the website, but I still have to type details about Eddie the lizard and Joey the greyhound. Tell me again about Hugo."

"We've had two phone calls," Caleb repeated.

"Ella, could you go and take over for Joel?" Heidi Harrison, Ella and Caleb's mom, broke in. "He's out in the stables with Mickey. Tell him there's a phone call for him."

Ella nodded. She was glad to break free from the computer and the chaos in the crowded room. "Hi, Grandpa!" She waved as she jogged across the yard.

"Hello! How's my favorite granddaughter?" He waved back.

"*Only* granddaughter!" she reminded him, laughing.

He grinned and headed toward the house. "Stop by if you get the time."

"Okay, I'll try!" Ella replied.

She found Joel, Animal Magic's veterinary assistant, spreading clean straw in Mickey's stable. "Joel, Mom says there's a phone call for you—hey, Mickey, get away from my shirt. It's not for eating!"

"Yum!" Joel laughed. He slipped a harness around the donkey's head and handed Ella the lead rope. "Do you want to take him out to the field?"

"Cool! Come on, Mickey," Ella said, careful now to avoid his big teeth.

Clip-clop. Mickey trotted happily across the yard, tugging Ella after him. They went out onto Main Street, then down the side road to the fields at the back of Animal Magic. "Ee-aawww!"

"Ouch!" Ella put her hands over her ears. "Not so loud!"

The donkey's ear-splitting bray brought Buttercup, Chance, and Rosie, the tiny Shetland pony, cantering up the hill.

Ella led Mickey through the gate and took off his harness. "Go play!" She watched him trot off with the three ponies. *If anyone gives Mickey a home, they're going to need earplugs!* she thought as she hurried back. She was about to return to the reception area when she remembered her grandpa and made a detour into the house.

"So, Ella-Bella, how are things?" he asked, cradling a cup of tea. Ella's dad sat next to him with his own "Best Dad in the World!" mug.

"Cool, Grandpa! We're really, *really* busy. We just found homes for Blossom and Cleo and maybe Hugo…. Hey, I just had a totally cool idea!"

"Uh-oh!" Grandpa glanced at his son, Mark. "Why is Ella looking at me with that mischievous look in her eye?"

"She *always* has that mischievous look in her eye," Dad joked.

Ella rolled her eyes and continued. "Grandpa, why don't *you* adopt Mickey?"

"Who's Mickey?"

"Don't ask, Dad!" Ella's dad warned. But it was too late.

"Mickey is a handsome donkey with long ears and ginormous eyes...."

"And a voice to match," Dad cut in.

Ella ignored her dad. "He's totally friendly and soft and cuddly, Grandpa. He wouldn't hurt a fly. And you've got that big empty field behind your garden center. There'd be plenty of room for Mickey there. He'd love it!"

"Say no," Dad advised.

"Da-ad!" Ella was angry now. "Do you want to find Mickey a home or not?"

"Yes, but it has to be the *right* home. Don't forget how busy Grandpa is. Besides, what would his neighbors say if Mickey woke them up at six every morning?"

Ella frowned. "Grandpa doesn't have

any neighbors," she pointed out. "Miss Elliot moved out. Her house is empty."

"Not anymore," Granpa told her. "A new family named Platt just moved in. They're fixing the old place up."

"Oh—well, I'm sure they'd like Mickey." Ella got the feeling she was losing the argument. It seemed that Mickey would have to stay on the Animal Magic website a little longer. "Gotta run—I promised Mom I'd help out!" she said. "But Grandpa, will you think about poor Mickey stuck here while everyone else is getting adopted? He's starting to think that no one wants him!"

"Cue the sad violins and take out your hankies!" Ella's dad sighed.

"Da-ad!" It was no good. "'Bye, Grandpa!" Ella said, giving him a quick

hug before hurrying back to the animal hospital.

That morning, Animal Magic took in three orphaned kittens, a ferret, two rabbits, and a gray, smooth-haired crossbreed puppy named Buster. They found a good new home for Val, as well as Blossom and Cleo.

"Working our magic!" As he sat at the computer, Caleb happily chanted the center's catchphrase. "To match the perfect pet with the perfect owner!"

Mom had finally closed the doors and stood at the desk with Joel, sorting through the paperwork. Meanwhile, Ella and Caleb were busy uploading photos of all the new animals onto the website.

"What a morning! Thanks, everyone." Mom glanced at her watch. "Come on— it's lunchtime!"

They were heading out into the yard when Joel dropped his bombshell. "Um, Heidi, there's something I need to talk to you about," he began awkwardly.

Mom shaded her eyes from the sun. "Does this have anything to do with your phone call earlier?"

Ella and Caleb turned and looked at Joel, who took a deep breath, then nodded.

"Yes, it was important."

"So?" an unsuspecting Ella asked.

Joel looked down at the ground. "It was about a new job I applied for. They made up their minds. It seems I got it."

"You want to leave Animal Magic?"
Ella gasped.

"I don't want to, but I am," Joel told
them. "At the end of this month, if that's
okay, Heidi?"

Chapter Two

Dalmatians on the Loose

"Australia!" Ella couldn't believe Joel's news. "It's hundreds of miles away. Why do you want to work there?"

It was early afternoon, and Joel was checking stock in the medicine cabinet. He checked off items on a long list and tried to explain. "The job is connected with the main veterinary school. I'll get to work with some amazing experts. And I'll learn a lot of new stuff."

"But what about us?" Ella sprayed tables in the operating room and wiped them clean. "Anyway, you could learn new stuff from Mom."

"No, I couldn't," Joel said firmly. "I've loved every minute here, Ella, but it's definitely time to broaden my horizons and move on."

Ella knew she would miss Joel. With his tall, gangly figure and mop of light brown hair, he'd been part of the Animal Magic team since it opened. Now he felt like part of the family. "Will you still come back and see us?" she asked.

"Just try and keep me away!" He grinned, picking up the phone. "Hello, Animal Magic ... oh, hi there, Jimmy. No, Heidi and Mark went out to run some errands. Ella's here, though. It's your grandpa," Joel said as he handed her the phone.

"Ella, there's a problem here at Gro-Well!" Grandpa sounded upset. "Two big dogs—Dalmatians—have escaped from the yard next door. They're destroying my plants!"

"Oh, no! Grandpa, I'm so sorry. Isn't anyone trying to stop them?"

"No. I've been over to the house, but there doesn't seem to be anyone home. I was wondering if there was someone at your place who could help me out?"

To get two rampaging dogs under control? You bet! "I'll find Caleb. We'll ride over right away," Ella promised.

"Find Caleb to do what?" Caleb

asked, wandering out of the cat area with one of the new kittens. "Where are you dragging me off to now?"

"Here, pass her to me." Quickly, Joel took the gray kitten from Caleb. "It's important, so don't ask questions—just follow Ella!"

Ella and Caleb rode their bikes up Main Street, out of the village toward their grandpa's small garden center.

"I've never heard him sound this upset before," Ella told her brother. "You know Grandpa—he's always so..."

"Happy?" Caleb chipped in.

Ella nodded. They flung down their bikes at the gates to the garden center and ran into the tiny office to find their grandpa on the phone.

"Mr. Platt? This is Jimmy Harrison from the garden center next door. Do you own a couple of Dalmatians? You do. Well, I'm glad I got a hold of you at last. Did you know your dogs have escaped from your yard? Yes, that's right. They're in my plants and doing terrible damage. So I'm hoping you'll be able ... Mr. Platt, are you there? Hello?"

"Don't worry, Grandpa, we'll catch them—no problem," Caleb promised, dashing outside.

Swiftly Ella followed him down the rows of upturned plants. "Wow, this is a mess!" she muttered.

Pots had been tipped over, spilling

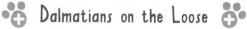

soil across the narrow paths. Plants lay crushed and broken. Suddenly, Ella spotted the first of the two dogs. "Over here!" she called to Caleb.

The black-and-white spotted dog was snapping at a green hose that curled across the path. Its ears were pricked, and it was pouncing as if the hose was a vicious snake.

"Down…. Sit!" Ella said in a stern voice.

The dog cocked her head to look at Ella, then pounced. She took the hose between her teeth and shook it hard.

Ella tried once more. "I said, down!" This time she used an arm movement that she and Caleb had learned at dog-training classes. With her palm facing inward, she crooked her forearm from the elbow and brought it up sharply toward her face. "Sit!"

The naughty dog saw her signal and obeyed.

"Good job!" Caleb muttered, spying the second runaway digging a deep hole in his grandpa's compost corner. He sprinted across and lunged at the dog, grabbing it by the collar.

The dog squirmed and dragged Caleb down, but he held on. When he stood up, his T-shirt and jeans were covered in wet, dark-brown compost.

"Nice tackle!" Ella called.

"I'm too slow these days," Grandpa complained, bringing strong rope for Ella and Caleb to use as dog leashes. "It's a good job you two are young and nimble."

Once on a leash, the two Dalmatians seemed to calm down. Ella and Caleb walked them back to Grandpa's office and commanded them to sit by the door.

"I've lost a lot of expensive plants," Grandpa sighed, stooping to stand the nearest large pot upright. "I'll definitely need to have a serious chat with my new neighbors about this."

Just then, a short, stocky man strode in through the entrance, closely followed by a girl about Ella's age. Both had fair, straight hair and gray eyes.

The man spotted the Dalmatians sitting quietly outside the office. "Bonnie, Clyde—there you are!"

"Mr. Platt?" Grandpa stepped forward. "We were speaking on the telephone. I think we were cut off."

The newcomer shook his head. "I was busy with something so I put the phone down. But in any case, we're here now. I'm Mike, and this is my daughter, Katie."

Um, how about saying sorry? Ella thought, glancing around at the ruined plants.

But Mr. Platt didn't seem like he was

going to apologize.

"I'd already been over to the
house before I called you," Grandpa
explained. "It seemed like there was
nobody keeping an eye on—er—Bonnie
and Clyde."

"As I said, I was busy." Mr. Platt
turned to his daughter. "Katie, run and
see if you can find where the dogs got
through the fence."

"I've already seen the broken planks,"
Ella said. She turned to the girl. "I can
show you if you like."

"Broken planks?" Mr. Platt echoed.
"Oh, well, if your fence is the problem,
I can't take any responsibility for my
dogs getting through."

Katie said nothing and looked down
at her feet.

"But that's not my fence," Grandpa objected. "It's yours."

Mr. Platt folded his arms and looked him in the eye. "I think you'll find, when you look into it, that the fence is yours, Mr. Harrison."

Yikes! Ella stared back at Katie. She

didn't like these new neighbors one bit.

"Well, there hasn't been a hole in it for as long as I've been here," Ella's grandpa argued back. "I think you let your dogs run out of control. They wrecked the fence, then broke through and ruined my plants!"

Mr. Platt clicked his tongue. "Here, Bonnie. Here, Clyde!"

The two strong Dalmatians stood up and strained at their leashes, dragging Caleb and Ella off their feet and forcing them to hand the ropes to Mr. Platt.

"My dogs are not out of control!" The new neighbor raised his voice.

"No way!" Katie agreed, standing up for her dad.

Ella and Caleb glared at her.

"So what do you call this?" Grandpa pointed at the wrecked plants.

"Not my problem," Mr. Platt said, setting off with his dogs. "If I were you, Mr. Harrison, I'd replace the fence so it doesn't happen again, or else."

"Or else what?" Grandpa called out after them.

"Or else you can expect a letter from my lawyer!" Mr. Platt yelled back as he marched through the gates.

"So the day turned out lousy," Ella grumbled to her dad once she was tucked in bed that night. "It was great at the beginning, getting Cleo and Blossom adopted and stuff, but then Joel said he was leaving, which is totally bad news, and now Grandpa finds out he's got the worst neighbors in the universe!"

"Don't worry. These things happen," Dad soothed. "I spoke to Grandpa and said I'd come over tomorrow morning to help him clean up the mess. Would you like to join us?"

From under her cozy comforter, Ella nodded. "Grandpa was really upset."

"Yes, well, it will cost him a lot of money to replace the plants and put up a new fence. And we're not even sure yet if it's his."

"Miss Elliot would never have made him do that."

"No. But she's moved out, and you have to realize that people are all different. Maybe Grandpa's new neighbors won't turn out to be so bad in the long run."

"They're horrible!" Ella insisted. "Just wait until you meet them. I'm never going to like them, Dad—that's for sure!"

Chapter Three
Ella's Discovery

Early the next morning, Mom sat at the computer in the reception area typing up the details for Joel's job. "Wanted— Veterinary Assistant. Animal Magic is looking for a well-qualified person to assist Veterinary Surgeon Heidi Harrison...."

"I wish Joel wasn't going," Ella sighed as she read the opening sentence. She glanced up and saw her dad beckoning to her through the window. "Oops,

I forgot—Dad and I are going to help
Grandpa clean up. Is that okay?"

Mom nodded. "Joel's due to start work
soon. And Caleb's around."

Ella grabbed some garbage bags,
brushes, and shovels from the stables
and piled them into the back of her
dad's van.

"We'll have the place cleaned up in
no time," Dad promised as they drove
out to Grandpa's garden center. "And if
we need to, we'll fix the fence so that it
doesn't happen again."

They parked outside the office, and
Ella leaped out. "Hi, Grandpa! What
do you want us to do first?"

Grandpa looked relieved to see them.
"We've got an hour before opening time.
If possible, I'd like to have everything

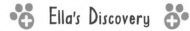

cleaned up before then."

So Grandpa, Dad, and Ella began scooping up the spilled soil and crushed plants and putting them on the compost heap.

"Do you want me to save the plastic labels?" Ella asked.

"Yes, please. Put them in the top drawer of the desk in my office," her grandpa replied. "You'll find a bunch of spare labels there."

"What about the fence?" Dad asked from outside the door.

Ella heard the two of them wander away, discussing how it could be fixed. Quickly she opened the drawer and slipped the labels in. Then she rushed outside again, eager to follow her dad and Grandpa.

But something made her stop. A tiny rustling noise was coming from the garbage can that stood by the office door. The can was used by Gro-well customers for candy and ice-cream wrappers and other pieces of garbage. It had a domed plastic top and a flap that swung in when you tapped it.

Rustle-rustle! Ella was sure that the noise was coming from inside the can. "What's that?" she muttered.

Scratch-scratch. Maybe something was trapped in there. Something too small to climb out by itself.... Gingerly Ella pushed at the flap and felt inside.

"Ouch!" She felt a sharp nip and pulled out her hand. "Ow!"

Luckily, when she looked at her finger

there was no blood.

Something's in there for sure, she thought. *And it's pretty scared; otherwise it wouldn't bite. It's tiny. A mouse or a baby squirrel, maybe.*

With her heart beating faster, she pulled off the lid of the garbage can and peered inside.

The can was almost full of litter, and at first Ella couldn't see the creature that had nipped her finger. All she could see were shiny chocolate wrappers, crushed potato chip bags, and old newspapers. *Wait a minute!*

There was a rolled-up newspaper near the top of the pile. Two tiny black eyes peered out of one end. Ella took a step closer and saw a brown face and a pair of round pink ears.

"A hamster!" Ella breathed. "Hello! What are you doing in here?"

At that second, the hamster saw Ella and shot back down the tunnel of newspaper. Quick as a flash, Ella lifted the roll out of the can and blocked both ends. The hamster was trapped inside.

"Dad!" she yelled. "Grandpa! Come quick!"

The two men had reached the far end of the garden center, but they came running when Ella called. "What's up?" her dad wanted to know.

"I found a hamster in the garbage

40

can!" she cried. "Somebody dumped him
and left him to die!"

Back at Animal Magic, Caleb brushed
up on hamster facts on the internet.
"Syrian hamster. Sometimes known
as golden hamster. Scientific name—
Mesocric … Mesocricetus…."

"*Auratus,*" Joel told him. He'd just
turned the rescued hamster upside down,
checked, and told them it was a male.

"So cute!" Ella said. "How could
anyone dump him as if he was garbage?"

"Syrian hamsters can grow up to 7
inches long," Caleb reported. "There are
short- and long-haired varieties. Colors
include golden, cream, cinnamon,
black…."

"This one is cinnamon banded," Joel told them confidently. "See—he has a broad white band of fur around his middle."

"Look at his little pink feet!" Ella cooed. "And his pink ears!"

"Bring him a cage," Joel told her. "You'll find one the right size in the storeroom outside the small animals unit. Spread plenty of wood shavings in the bottom, and make sure that you fill a water bottle for him. He's bound to be thirsty after his adventure."

"I wonder how long he was in the garbage can," Caleb muttered.

Holding the hamster carefully in the palm of his hand, Joel gently petted him. "He's certainly used to being handled. Nice and tame. Doesn't bite."

"Want to bet?" Ella asked as she brought back the cage. "He bit me when I first put my hand in the garbage can!"

"What do you expect? You'd bite, too, if a giant hand suddenly tried to grab you!" Caleb said, grinning.

"I think he's been well taken care of," Joel insisted. "So it's a mystery how he came to end up in the garbage can."

"Anyway, what are we going to name him?" Already Caleb was planning the wording for the website entry—"Syrian hamster. Owner didn't want him. Lonely and looking for a loving home."

Ella petted the tiny hamster with the tip of her forefinger. "He needs a cute name so people will notice him."

"Goldie," Joel suggested. "Peter, Fred, Hammy?"

But Ella shook her head. "None of those suit him."

Gently Joel lowered the newcomer into his cage and closed the door. The hamster blinked, then scampered toward the water bottle.

"How about Hamlet?" Caleb suggested.

"Hamlet?" As Ella tested it out, the little hamster turned his head and twitched his ears. "Hamlet!" Ella laughed. "He likes it. Hamlet it is!"

Chapter Four

Turning Detective

"Dumped!" Ella insisted to Annie
Brooks. She was sitting on her
neighbor's fence, watching Mickey graze
alongside Rosie, Buttercup, and Chance.
The mare and her foal belonged to the
Brooks family. Rosie, the little Shetland,
was staying at Animal Magic until
they found a home for her, but she and
Mickey were allowed to share the field.

Annie was amazed. "You mean the
hamster was just dropped into your

grandpa's garbage can and left there?"

"Left to die!" Ella frowned and shook her head. "I'm surprised the shock didn't kill poor Hamlet. And if I hadn't found him when I did, he would soon have starved or ended up in a landfill! He's okay now, though. Joel checked him out, and we gave him a nice comfy cage."

In the distance Mickey raised his head and let out an ear-splitting bray. The ponies kicked up their heels and galloped to a safe distance.

"So who dumped Hamlet?" Annie asked.

Ella shrugged. "I don't know. But I'm going to find out. Do you want to help?"

Annie nodded. "Where do we start?"

"At Grandpa's place. We'll pick up the trail from the start. Right now!"

Annie jumped from the fence into her backyard. "I'll just tell Mom where we're going," she said. "Wait here. I'll be back in a second."

"You're welcome to try, but I think you've got a difficult job on your hands." Grandpa had listened patiently to Ella and Annie's plan, but now he shook his head. "It could have been any one of a hundred people who dropped the poor little thing into the can. I had a lot of customers yesterday."

"I know that, Grandpa, but I hoped you'd be able to remember a few details." Ella wasn't discouraged. She was determined to identify Hamlet's owner. "For instance, when did you last empty the garbage can?"

"And was there anyone hanging around yesterday who looked suspicious?" Annie added.

Ella's grandpa wrinkled his nose. "Let me see. Oh, you mean the man wearing the black mask and the striped sweater, carrying a sack over his shoulder...."

"Grandpa!" Ella groaned. "It's important. We want to find out who did this to poor Hamlet, and make sure they don't do it again."

"So you're turning into Sherlock Holmes." Grandpa sat down at the counter. "Okay, let me think. Most of yesterday's customers were locals I know well. I don't think any of them would be likely to abandon Hamlet."

"What about the customers you

didn't know?" Ella asked. "Was anyone hanging around near the garbage can?" As she quizzed her grandpa, she saw someone hovering outside the entrance. It was Katie Platt, half hidden by a tall tree, but peeking around at Ella, then ducking out of sight when she realized she'd been spotted.

"Hang on a minute." Her grandpa broke off to serve a customer.

"Did you see that?" Ella whispered to Annie. "Katie Platt is spying on us!"

"Katie who?" Annie hadn't heard about the new family at Miss Elliot's old house.

Just then, Katie leaned back into view, then quickly ducked out of sight again.

"That's her!" Ella hissed. "You must know who I mean. She's the new girl in

Mr. Hawke's class at school."

"Oh, yeah, her," Annie nodded.

"What's she up to? Why is she hiding?" Ella muttered.

Annie had no time to answer before a dark-haired woman in white pants and a bright-pink shirt appeared in the entrance.

"Come on, Katie, don't hang back. Bring Bonnie and Clyde with you!" the woman said as she approached the counter where Grandpa had just finished serving a customer.

Reluctantly the fair-haired girl

appeared from behind the tree with the
two Dalmatians. They wagged their
tails and tugged Katie along, sniffing
into every corner.

"Mr. Harrison?" the woman said in a
friendly voice.

"That's me," Ella's grandpa answered
curtly, gearing up for another argument.

"I'm Julia Platt, your new neighbor. I
believe you've already met my husband,
Mike, and Katie, plus our two dogs."

"You could say that," Grandpa
sniffed. "We didn't get off to a very good
start, I'm afraid."

Mrs. Platt nodded. "Katie told me
all about Bonnie and Clyde and the
damage they caused. I felt I should stop
by to apologize."

Wow! Ella stared at Mrs. Platt, then at

Katie, who still looked as if she didn't
want to be there.

"My husband has a lot on his mind
right now," Mrs. Platt went on. "Our
move didn't go as smoothly as we'd
hoped, and yesterday we had to deal
with a broken boiler and no plumber
would come out on a Saturday—well,
all I can say is that, frankly, Mike was
not in the best of moods!"

Grandpa nodded. "That's all right.
We won't worry any more about the
incident with the dogs. We've cleaned
everything up, and my son and I are
sure we can fix the fence, no problem."

"But you must let me pay for the
damage!" Where her husband had
been rude and unreasonable, Mrs. Platt
was sweet and helpful. "And I have

to apologize again about Bonnie and Clyde's behavior. They're young dogs, you see, and we only recently got them from an animal rescue center in our old town. It turns out they hadn't been well trained by their previous owner."

By now Ella's grandpa was nodding and smiling, and the two grown-ups were getting along nicely. Only Katie still looked uncomfortable as she made the Dalmatians stand by the garbage can, keeping them on a tight leash.

"You should talk to my granddaughter here," Grandpa was telling Mrs. Platt. "I'm sure Ella and her brother, Caleb, would be able to help you with your dogs. They often train animals at Animal Magic, down on Main Street."

"Did you hear that, Katie?" Mrs.

Platt turned to her daughter. "Doesn't that sound like a good idea?"

Katie shrugged while Bonnie and Clyde pulled restlessly at their leashes. They tugged so hard that Katie fell sideways against the garbage can. The whole thing toppled to the ground.

Woof-woof! The startled dogs strained at their leashes and broke free. They fled through the garden center gates.

"Oh, no, not again!" Katie sighed. She ran to catch Bonnie and Clyde.

"Oh, dear!" Mrs. Platt sighed. "I'm beginning to think those dogs are more trouble than they're worth. The things is, Katie is crazy about animals—cats, dogs, rabbits, hamsters, you name it."

"Really?" Ella was surprised. Katie didn't come across as the kind of kid who was crazy about animals.

"Yes. Believe me, she'd be heartbroken if we let Bonnie and Clyde go."

Woof-woof! The two Dalmatians had raced next door and were rampaging across the yard.

"Come here! Sit! Lie down!" a desperate Katie cried.

"Did you say hamsters?" A sudden suspicion flashed into Ella's mind.

"Yes. Anything with fur and four legs." Mrs. Platt smiled wearily. She got ready to lend her daughter a hand with the boisterous dogs.

"So does Katie have any other pets?" Ella asked, blocking Mrs. Platt's way. "Like a hamster, for instance? Does she have a hamster?"

"Why, yes!" Mrs. Platt said. Then she frowned. "Actually, no, not right now."

Yes or no? Which is it? Surely Mrs. Platt must know.

"I'm sorry, but I'd better get back next door to catch those dogs!" Mrs. Platt said as she stepped past Ella.

"What color is Katie's hamster?" Ella called after her.

But Mrs. Platt was in too much of a hurry to answer.

Chapter Five

Searching for a Home

"I bet I'm right!" Ella told Annie.

"But you can't be sure," Annie argued. Ella had been explaining her Hamlet theory all the way back from the garden center.

"You must admit that it looks pretty suspicious." Ella headed for the reception area, where Mom was reading through the first applications for Joel's job.

"Ella thinks it was Katie Platt who dumped Hamlet," Annie told Mom.

"Uh-oh, is Ella playing detective again?" Ella's mom was too busy to pay much attention.

"Of course!" Annie grinned. "Anyway, now she's going to introduce me."

"That's nice," Mom muttered. She clicked the mouse and read some details: "Jen Andrews. Age 26, trained in Dublin, special qualification in dental nursing. Hmm."

"Here he is, right at the end!" Ella announced, leading Annie into the small animals unit. The rabbits, hamsters, guinea pigs, and mice were lined up in clean, bright cages, each with a water bottle and a dish of special food.

Annie followed Ella down the row of squeaking, burrowing creatures. They passed Hugo the friendly brown rabbit up at the bars of his cage, then Honey and Happy, two harlequin bunnies with black patches on their gray fur and black pom-pom tails. Then there were Lulu and Lacy, the long-haired guinea pigs, and Frankie the ferret, peeking shyly out of his nest of straw.

At the end of the row, Ella carefully opened Hamlet's cage. She reached in and picked him up.

Little Hamlet blinked and twitched his ears. He sniffed at Ella's fingers and decided he was perfectly happy sitting in the palm of her hand.

"Can I hold him?" Annie asked excitedly.

Ella handed over the hamster.

His little pink feet felt funny and scratchy, and his brown and white furry body was soft and warm. "Will he bite?" Annie asked.

"Not if you're gentle and don't make him jump." Hamlet seemed used to people, and not easily scared, even after his ordeal in the garbage can. "He's cute, isn't he?"

"Adorable!" Annie grinned. She pursed her lips and pretend-kissed the hamster. "Is he on the website yet?"

Ella nodded. "Caleb put him up as soon as we'd chosen his name."

"So, even if you're right about Katie Platt, you don't want to send him back to her?"

"No way!" Ella took Hamlet from Annie and placed him back in his cage. Then she went to the fridge and took a slice of apple from a plastic container.

"Hamster treat coming up!"

"But if Katie is Hamlet's real owner, shouldn't you tell her where he is?" Annie saw trouble ahead if Ella forged on and found Hamlet a new home.

Ella pushed the slice of apple through the bars of Hamlet's cage, then shook her head. She was one hundred percent sure that her theory was right. "Katie abandoned him, didn't she? She *so* doesn't want him back!"

"Even so." Annie felt uncomfortable. "Maybe she had a reason."

"Such as?" Ella couldn't see it. "You saw what she was like, Annie. She doesn't take care of her pets. That's why Hamlet is not going back to her."

End of story. No ifs or buts.

At school on Monday, Ella told as many people as possible about Hamlet the abandoned hamster, hoping to find him a new home.

"He's really cute and friendly," she told Miss Jennings, her teacher. "And so easy to take care of."

"I'm sorry, Ella," Miss Jennings said with a smile. "I can't possibly give Hamlet a home. I go away to my house in Florida every school vacation. Who would take care of him while I was away?"

"Hamlet is brown and white, with furry ears and pink feet." Ella described the hamster to Mrs. Owen, one of the cafeteria workers at Lakewood

Elementary. "He doesn't bite, and he likes to be held."

Mrs. Owen stopped stacking up the dishes and listened carefully. "We did have a hamster a long time ago," she said.

"They're so easy to take care of," Ella rushed on. "You only have to clean out their cages and give them fresh water and food. If you give them a wheel to play in, that's all the exercise they need!"

Mrs. Owen nodded. "I know. But my son, Matthew, is grown up now, so we don't have any pets. Besides, they make my husband sneeze if he's in the same room as them. So no, Ella, I'm afraid I can't give Hamlet a home."

That afternoon on the way home, Annie sympathized with Ella on the school bus. "It's okay. You tried."

Ella sighed and stared out the window at the bushes and fields beyond. "Trying isn't enough. Honestly, Annie, I've got to find a home for Hamlet before…."

"…Before Katie Platt finds out where he is, changes her mind, and decides she wants him back?" Annie guessed. "I'd ask Mom if we could have Hamlet, but I'm sure she'll say no."

Linda Brooks had already adopted

Buttercup and Chance from Animal
Magic and was letting Rosie and
Mickey graze in her field. Annie knew
that asking her mom to adopt Hamlet
would be one step too far.

As the bus pulled up at the Crystal
Park stop, Annie and Ella got off with
the other kids.

"George, do you want to adopt a
hamster?" Ella pounced on her brother's
best friend, who had already given a
home to Lucky the rabbit.

"Nope," he said, brushing her aside
and heading up Three Oaks Road with
Emma Matthews.

Caleb overheard and tutted. "I
already asked George."

"Tell your mom about Hamlet
anyway," Ella muttered to Annie as

they said good-bye on Main Street.

Inside Ella and Caleb's house, Mom was still going through job applications. She'd had five so far. "Which of these would you choose to interview?" she asked Caleb and Ella, showing them the printouts. "Oh, by the way, I got a phone call from Julia Platt about Bonnie and Clyde. I told her you'd both be glad to help with dog-training classes for those two rascals."

"You what!" Ella gasped.

"Ella, speak properly," Mom told her. "It's not 'you what,' it's 'excuse me' if you didn't hear properly, although I'm sure you did."

"The Platts aren't exactly Ella's favorite family," Caleb explained. "But I bet training the dogs would be cool.

When do we start?"

"Tonight before dinner," Mom said, still sifting through her papers. "In fact, you'd better head over now. I told Mrs. Platt you'd be there by five."

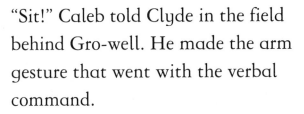

"Sit!" Caleb told Clyde in the field behind Gro-well. He made the arm gesture that went with the verbal command.

The young Dalmatian sat down on the grass.

Click! Caleb pressed the small training clicker, then swiftly handed Clyde a tasty treat. Click-and-treat. It worked like magic.

Ella stood with Bonnie until Clyde had gotten the hang of the "Sit" command. Once, twice, three times.

"Good boy!" Caleb patted the dog's broad head.

Clyde wagged his tail and licked his lips.

"Now it's our turn," Ella told Bonnie, who immediately leaped up and ran across the field, skipping and jumping and acting wild.

"Crazy!" Caleb sighed.

But Ella wasn't easily beaten. "Here, Bonnie!" She held up a doggie treat.

Bonnie recognized food from far away. Barking happily, she bounded back to Ella.

"Sit!" Ella ordered as the dog screeched to a halt. Voice and arm gesture together. Be firm. Say it again. "Sit!"

Bonnie obeyed. *Click* went Ella's clicker. Then the reward. *Gulp*! Bonnie swallowed it down.

"Again," Caleb said quietly.

Ella repeated the exercise patiently and firmly. After six commands and six successes, she was happy. "Good girl!" she said, patting Bonnie. "You're a beautiful dog. Yes, you are!"

Happy Bonnie loved the attention. She gazed up at Ella, waiting for the next command.

"Okay, let's try 'Stay,'" Caleb decided. "'Sit' and 'Stay.' If Bonnie and Clyde get that far in one session, they'll be doing well."

And sure enough, the young Dalmatians were smart dogs who learned easily. After half an hour of click-and-treat, Ella and Caleb walked them back home with high hopes.

"How did it go?" Mrs. Platt asked them as they ushered the dogs into the house.

Caleb let Clyde off the leash while Ella dried Bonnie's feet with an old towel.

"They did really well," Caleb told Mrs. Platt. "We taught 'Sit' and 'Stay.'"

Next time we'll try 'Come here.'"

"You hear that, Katie?" Mrs. Platt called over her shoulder.

As usual, Katie Platt was lurking behind the nearest large object. At her mother's urging, she edged out from behind the door.

"Bonnie and Clyde just had their first training session and they passed with flying colors!" her mom said.

Katie frowned and said nothing.

Giving Bonnie one last wipe with the towel, Ella let her go. The dog bounced off toward Katie and began to tug at the hem of her jeans. She was soon joined by Clyde, and the two dogs jumped up at Katie, who seemed helpless to stop them. "Down!" she ordered, but the dogs ignored her, so she turned and stomped off into the house.

"I'm worried about Katie," Mrs. Platt said as if she was thinking out loud. "She doesn't seem to be settling into Crystal Park or her new school very well. I think she misses her old friends."

Caleb nodded and blushed. There was an awkward silence.

Meanwhile, Ella's eyes wandered across the junk piled up in the storage room. There were cardboard boxes everywhere, and plastic lawn chairs stacked in a corner. On top of the chairs there was a small, empty animal cage.

"Hey!" Ella said under her breath.

"Well, see you tomorrow," Caleb was saying to Mrs. Platt.

"Yes, and thank you for agreeing to train Bonnie and Clyde. It's such a relief."

Ella double-checked the cage. It was tipped on its end, with wood shavings spilling out through the bars. And there was a metal wheel and a water bottle and everything a hamster would need.

"Caleb!" Ella ran to catch up with him out on the road. "Wait for me. Guess what I just saw!"

"I don't know, but I bet you're going to tell me."

"An empty hamster cage perched on top of the lawn chairs."

"So?" Caleb asked, putting on his helmet and picking up his bike.

"So that's the proof we needed about Hamlet. He *did* live here with Katie Platt, and no wonder she looks so guilty all the time. She so totally *is* the person who dumped Hamlet!"

Chapter Six
First Impressions

Ella's suspicions about Katie Platt had
turned into concrete certainty.

"It's obvious when you think about
it," she explained to Annie on Tuesday
morning. "She must've already decided
to get rid of Hamlet when she came to
Grandpa's garden center with her dad.
She was most likely keeping him hidden
in her pocket, waiting for her chance.
And when her dad was getting mad at
Grandpa about the fence, she happened

to be standing next to the garbage can,
so she just flipped the lid and dropped
poor Hamlet in."

"But why?" Annie asked. She and Ella
had been waiting in the lunch line when
Ella spotted Katie Platt standing alone
at the cafeteria door.

"Quiet!" Ella warned.

"Why would Katie want to get rid of
her hamster?" Annie whispered.

"Maybe she was tired of taking care
of him," Ella suggested. "At Animal
Magic, we're used to people getting
bored and dumping their pets—it
happens all the time. They're all
into it at first, then they just can't be
bothered."

Annie frowned. "But her mom said
Katie loved animals."

"I'm not so sure." Ella noticed Katie wander across the cafeteria to join the line, so she shushed Annie again.

"Stand in line," Mrs. Owen told everyone, making a space for Katie behind Annie and Ella. "You're new, aren't you, dear? Whose class are you in?"

"Mr. Hawke's," Katie mumbled.

Just then Mrs. Owen spotted Ella. "Oh, hello, Ella. I'm glad to see you," she said in her loud, cheery voice. "I mentioned Hamlet the hamster to my son, Matthew."

Ella drew a deep breath and frowned. For once she didn't want to talk about Hamlet—not with Katie listening.

Mrs. Owen chatted on. "It turns out that Matthew would love to have a

hamster for his own little boy, Kyle.
He's thinking of bringing Kyle out to
Animal Magic this weekend to take a
look at little Hamlet."

Ella nodded. *Talk about something else!*

By now Katie was taking in every
word, biting her lip and looking more
unhappy.

"What color is Hamlet?" Mrs. Owen
asked, reaching behind Ella's back to
get a plate for Katie.

*Nightmare! Change the subject. Can't you
see—I don't want Katie to know!* But Mrs.
Owen wasn't picking up on any of the
signals. On she went.

"And how did the poor thing end up at
the rescue center in the first place?"

Before Ella could clear her throat to
give an answer, Annie nudged her with

her elbow. "Ahem!"

Ella turned, just in time to see tears welling up in Katie Platt's gray eyes.

Mrs. Owen noticed, too. "Oh, dear!" she muttered as Katie turned and dashed out of the cafeteria. "Was it something I said?"

"Kyle Owen." Caleb made a note of the name. "You say he's coming in to see Hamlet this weekend?"

"I hope!" Ella told him. It was already Thursday evening, and Mrs. Owen had spoken to Ella again about her grandson and how much he wanted to have a pet. "So keep your fingers crossed!"

"Who are we keeping our fingers crossed about now?" Mom had just come into the reception area with a stranger—a tall, thin-faced woman with fashionable jet-black hair, dressed in jeans and a red sweater.

"Hamlet," Ella answered. "We might have found the perfect owner."

"Matching the perfect pet with the

perfect owner!" The woman obviously knew the Animal Magic motto. She smiled as she said it, and her serious face was transformed. Her gray eyes shone, and her lips parted to show perfect white teeth.

"Ella, Caleb, this is Jen Andrews—she applied for Joel's job, so she's here to take a look around."

Ella's "hello" was guarded, but Caleb shook Jen's hand. "Do you want me to show you the cat area?" he offered.

"Yes, that sounds good," Jen said, eagerly following Caleb out of the reception area.

"Maybe you could show her around the small animals unit afterward," Mom suggested to Ella. "I've already shown her the kennels. She seems nice."

"Okay," Ella agreed. But it seemed odd to be showing Jen around when Joel was still here—as if she was helping to shove him out.

"How many small animals do you have right now?" Jen asked after Caleb had done his part of the tour. She was following Ella down the row of rabbits and guinea pigs toward the cage at the end.

"Twenty," Ella told her. "I like them all, but Hamlet is my favorite."

Jen stooped to look into Hamlet's cage. "Yes, he's a handsome little fellow," she agreed. "Can I hold him?"

Ella nodded. She opened the cage and scooped up Hamlet.

"He's quite perky, isn't he?" Jen smiled as she handled him. "Does he have a regular grooming routine?"

Ella nodded. "His nails are a little too long, though. I'm going to ask Mom or Joel to clip them."

"Good idea." Inspecting Hamlet carefully, Jen's smile faded a little. "Hmm, Hamlet's eyes are a little watery. Have you noticed?"

"No. Is that bad?" Suddenly Ella was anxious.

"Could be. Has Hamlet had much soft food since he came in?"

Ella thought for a moment. "I give him apples as a treat. Does that count?"

Jen nodded and pressed gently against the hamster's cheeks. "Sometimes soft food gets stuck way back in the cheek pouches. It presses against the tear ducts and makes their eyes water."

"I didn't know that!" Ella gasped. "Poor Hamlet—he's sick and it's all my fault!"

"Don't worry—it's not serious," said Jen. "But it makes him uncomfortable. What we need is a tiny eyedropper filled with warm water that we can drop into Hamlet's mouth to flush out the pouches."

Ella nodded and went quickly to the

storeroom to get the dropper. Soon Jen was holding open Hamlet's mouth while Ella gently dropped in the liquid.

"There!" With her little finger Jen eased the food out of the hamster's cheek pouches. "That's better, isn't it?"

Ella nodded and sighed. *What a relief!* "How come you know so much about hamsters?" she asked.

Smiling, Jen put Hamlet back in his cage. "I made a special study of small rodents when I was in college—especially illnesses having to do with their mouths and teeth."

"Cool!" Ella watched as Hamlet climbed inside his wheel and began trotting around and around. "Really, Jen—thanks. Hamlet's totally happy now, thanks to you!"

Chapter Seven

Second Chances

"Jen Andrews gets Ella's vote," Mom told Joel. It was Saturday morning, and she and Joel were on the porch outside the reception area talking about the applicants for Joel's job. "She can hardly wait to shove you out the door!"

"That's not true!" Ella yelled as she set off across the yard on her bike. "I still want Joel to stay, but if we have to have someone new, I want it to be Jen!"

"No one could ever accuse Ella of holding back her opinion!" Mom laughed, watching her daughter follow Caleb up Main Street.

It was time for another session with Bonnie and Clyde, and Ella was looking forward to it. *As long as we don't see Katie*, she thought. All week at school she'd been avoiding her, and at their nightly training sessions, Ella had been glad when Katie wasn't around.

"Don't you think you're being a bit hard on the poor girl?" Ella's grandpa had asked after the Friday evening lesson. He'd been watching from his side of the fence and had seen Ella deliberately turn away from Katie when Mrs. Platt brought her out to watch.

"No way!" Ella had said. "Grandpa, it

was Katie who dumped Hamlet in your garbage can, remember? How can I be friends with someone as cruel as that?"

Overnight, Grandpa had been thinking about what Ella had said, and this morning he stopped her as she and Caleb arrived at the Platt's house.

"Hello, Ella-Bella," he greeted her. "How's my favorite...."

"I'm in a hurry, Grandpa!" she called. "Bonnie and Clyde are waiting for us!"

Sure enough, the Dalmatians had heard her voice and set up a duet of excited barks and yelps from the Platt's screened-in porch.

"I just need a quick word with you," Grandpa said.

Oops! Ella guessed she was in trouble. "What did I do wrong?"

"Nothing," he assured her, taking off his thick gardening gloves and rolling back his sleeves. "It's not what you *have* done—more what you *haven't* done!"

"What do you mean?" Ella asked.

"You haven't made friends with Katie," Grandpa explained. "And I think maybe you've been a bit hasty."

"Oh!" Ella frowned. She thought she'd explained all that.

Her grandfather pressed on. "Katie seems pretty unhappy," he pointed out.

Sulky—yes. Bad tempered—definitely. But unhappy?

"Think about it," her grandfather went on. "She's just moved to a new house and a new school with hundreds of new people. And her mom and dad are too busy with the house to help her settle in properly. How would you feel if you were her?"

"Grandpa," Ella protested. "You missed one big thing—Katie Platt has been cruel to Hamlet. She dumped him, and he could have died!"

There was a long pause while Grandpa rubbed his chin. "Maybe so," he said quietly. "But you don't know for sure that it was Katie, and even so, Ella, I think you should give her a second chance."

"Sit!" "Stay!" "Come here!" Ella and Caleb ran through the commands.

As usual, Bonnie and Clyde were A students.

"Nice work!" Grandpa called from his rows of sweet peas and roses.

"You'd never know they were the same dogs!" Mr. Platt, who'd come out of the house, praised what he saw.

"What did I tell you?" Mrs. Platt joined him as Caleb and Ella went on with the lesson. "Come and look, Katie. See how well the dogs are doing!"

Katie trailed out of the house to stare blankly over the fence into the field beyond.

"Now we'll do 'Fetch!'" Ella decided,

setting a stick in the grass. She told
Bonnie to sit and stay.

Bonnie fidgeted as she gazed at the
tempting stick beside her. She pricked her
ears, then looked up at Ella, who had
walked 20 steps across the field.

"Okay. Now, 'Fetch!'" Ella called.

Quick as a flash, Bonnie grabbed the
stick and raced toward Ella.

"Great!" Click-and-treat. "Good girl!"

That afternoon, Ella and Annie came
up with a plan to saddle Buttercup and
ride her down to the river.

"We want to see if Buttercup likes
to paddle," Ella told Mom, who was
busy at the computer. "Some horses like
water, don't they?"

"Yes, and some don't," Mom warned. "When I was young, I had a pony who wouldn't even go near a puddle." She glanced up as the door to the reception area opened and Mrs. Platt walked in with two lively customers. "Hello! What can we do for Bonnie and Clyde?" she asked with a pleasant smile.

"We'd like you to microchip them," Mrs. Platt explained, holding the door open for Katie, who trailed after her. "We knew when we adopted them that they would need chipping."

The Dalmatians padded around the tiled floor, poking into every corner.

"No problem," Mom assured Mrs. Platt. "Have a seat while I get things ready in the treatment room."

"Okay, Mom, I'm off to find Annie!"

Ella said hastily. She didn't even glance at Katie as she left.

But she was only halfway across the yard when she remembered Buttercup's treat and made a dash for the storeroom outside the small animals unit.

Ella fished around in a cardboard box and picked out the juiciest apple. She was just heading back when she heard a movement from inside the unit. *Better make sure that everything is okay*, she thought, and pushed open the door.

Katie Platt had sneaked in and was tiptoeing down the row of cages and gazing in. When she came to Hamlet's cage, she crouched down low.

Ella watched in amazement. *How can she face him after what she did to him?*

Katie did nothing except stare at

cuddly, easygoing Hamlet. The hamster poked his pink nose through the bars of his cage and twitched his whiskers.

"Ahhh!" Katie said softly.

Then Mom and Mrs. Platt came to find her.

"Ella, I thought you'd gone riding," Mom said, squeezing past.

"I am—I forgot Buttercup's apple!" Ella stammered.

"Ah, Katie, there you are." Mrs. Platt spied her daughter by Hamlet's cage. Her smile faded. "Time to go," she said sadly.

Katie's lip trembled, and she put her hand up to the bars of Hamlet's cage. "'Bye!" she whispered, following her mom back into the reception area.

Chapter Eight

Love at First Sight

That evening Ella was serious and silent.

"What's up? You haven't said a word for at least five minutes. Are you sick?" Caleb asked after dinner.

"Yes, sick of you asking silly questions," Ella grumbled. Annie had said the same thing out on the ride— was Ella okay? Had something bad happened at Animal Magic?

"No, everything's cool," Ella had told her.

But she couldn't figure it out. Why had Katie Platt snuck in to see Hamlet?

And why had she looked as if she was about to cry?

I get it! she thought suddenly as she put on her pajamas and brushed her teeth. *Katie abandoned Hamlet and now she's feeling guilty! She had to make sure it was him and that he was okay. But now she's feeling really bad!*

Mystery solved. Ella went to bed feeling better. At least Katie Platt wasn't a total monster after all.

Ella got up the next morning full of energy, with high hopes that the sunny Sunday would bring in a lot of people wanting to adopt pets.

"I've got a feeling it's going to be a good day!" she told Caleb, who was updating the website. "I bet we find homes for at least five of our animals."

"That would be an amazing day," Caleb muttered. "In fact, you'd probably need to wave a magic wand to get five in one day."

"Ha ha, you're funny." *Typical Caleb.* "First off, Mickey—I've decided I'm going to ask Annie's mom to take him."

Caleb grunted. "I wouldn't hold my breath. Face it, Ella—Mrs. Brooks is more likely to adopt Rosie than Mickey."

"She likes Mickey!" Ella protested. "Yesterday I saw her in the field petting him and giving him a carrot."

"Who else?" Caleb challenged.

"Hugo," Ella decided. "I bet one of

those people who called about him comes in."

"And?"

"Hamlet!" she declared. "Mrs. Owen's grandson will want him the minute he sees him." There was no more time to convince Caleb before the first people arrived.

"We'd like a dog," a middle-aged couple explained to Joel. "We've just lost our beloved Sandy. Now we're looking for a dog that's already house-trained."

"How about Buster?" Ella broke in. "And Penny's very friendly. Would you like to look at them?"

The couple nodded and followed Joel and Ella into the noisy kennels. Within minutes they'd fallen in love with Buster and decided he was the dog for them.

"Success!" Ella reported to Caleb when she went back into the reception area. She spotted a man and a small curly-haired boy reading flyers in the rack. "Is your name Kyle Owen?" she asked the boy eagerly. "Have you come about a hamster? Follow me!"

The boy and his dad went with Ella into the small animals unit.

"Your grandma sent you, didn't she? I told her all about Hamlet. He's right at the end of the row." Ella led the way, talking all the while.

"Wow!" Little Kyle was amazed by each animal he came to. He liked the rabbits and the guinea pigs. "They're cool. What are they?" he asked, pointing to Honey and Happy. "I like this one!" he cried, stopping by Frankie the ferret's cage.

"Hamlet's down here," Ella insisted.

But Kyle was staring in wonderment
at Frankie, who was sitting by the bars,
raised up on his haunches, his front paws
dangling. "What's his name?"

"That's Frankie. He's a ferret," Ella said.

"Look how fast he moves," he said to
his dad as the ferret darted to the back of
his cage and burrowed in his straw bed.
"Look—his face is peeking out."

"Do you like him?" Matthew Owen
asked with a smile.

Ella frowned. This wasn't supposed to be happening. But then again, it would be great if Frankie found a new home. "Um, would you like to see Hamlet before you decide?" she asked quietly.

"I like this one, Dad!" Kyle's eyes were shining. "Can I have him?"

And that was it—love at first sight. Ferret or hamster—it didn't matter to Kyle. Matthew Owen filled out the forms, and he and Kyle took Frankie home.

"I'm sorry, Hamlet," Ella said to her favorite hamster when she returned. "You're still homeless, but don't worry— I'm sure it won't be for long."

Hamlet ambled up and sniffed at her hand. Then he went back to his squeaky wheel. *I'm not worried*, he seemed to say. *I'm perfectly happy here, thank you very much!*

Chapter Nine
The Runaway Dog

"Hugo is really tame and friendly,"
Caleb was telling a woman named
Martha Shaw, who had come to Animal
Magic with her twin daughters, Leanne
and Beth.

He'd carried Hugo's cage into the
reception area and put it on the desk.
Mrs. Shaw lifted each girl to peer inside.

The brown rabbit flicked his long ears.
He crept forward to the bars, wrinkling
his nose and twitching his whiskers.

The twins smiled and giggled.

"He's perfect," they said. "Can we have him?"

"Yes, if you promise to take turns feeding him and cleaning his hutch," their mom agreed.

"And give him lots of cuddles," Ella added. She'd seen how well things were going and was hovering by the computer, ready to take Hugo off the website.

"We promise!" the girls chorused.

So Caleb and Ella gave the twins some flyers about how to care for a rabbit while Joel took the family's details.

"This is incredible!" Ella cried after the Shaws had left with Hugo. She danced around the waiting area, pretending to wave a magic wand. It was only three o'clock, and they were having amazingly good luck. "Who says we can't find homes for five pets in one day!"

"Hugo, Buster, Frankie," Caleb counted the names on his fingers. "Duh! That's only three."

"Someone else is coming in to visit the kennels in half an hour," she reminded him. "Mom said they were interested in a Jack Russell, and we've got Gus."

"Which will make four, not five," Caleb said stubbornly.

Ella frowned and thought hard. "Wait here!" she said, dashing outside.

She ran next door and found Annie and her dad sitting in the sunshine. "Hi, Mr. Brooks. Hi, Annie. Where's your mom?"

"Out in the field with the ponies. Why?" Annie looked up from her book.

"Nothing. I just need to see her."

Quickly Ella slipped through the back gate into the pony field, where she spotted Mrs. Brooks busily pulling up weeds by the fence.

"Hi, Buttercup! Hi, Chance!" Ella said, pausing to pet the gray mare and her foal. She gave Rosie a quick pat, then put her hands to her ears as Mickey gave his ear-splitting greeting. "Ouch, Mickey! Nice to see you, too!"

The noise made Mrs. Brooks look up. "Hello, Ella!" She waved.

Ella jogged over to join her.

"I'm digging up ragwort," Mrs. Brooks explained. "I don't want to run the risk of Buttercup and the rest eating it."

"No way!" Ella was happy to help dig up the poisonous weed. She tugged at the roots and threw the plants into the bucket. "So how are Buttercup and Chance today?" she asked casually.

"Fine, thanks."

"And Rosie?"

"Rosie's doing fine as well. Have you found anyone who wants a beautiful little Shetland pony yet?"

Ella shook her head. "No, but we will soon. And how's Mickey?"

"Ee-aww!" The donkey kicked up his heels and cantered across the field.

"Fine." Mrs. Brooks looked hard at Ella. "What are you up to?" she asked.

"I'm helping you with the ragwort," she said innocently.

"No, really—I'm getting a strong feeling that you *want* something."

Ella took a deep breath, then stood up. "Okay, you're right. I do. It's about

Mickey. He's sweet, isn't he?"

"'Sweet' is not quite the word I'd use."

"But you like him?"

"I wouldn't say 'like' exactly, either."

"He makes you laugh?" Ella persisted. "He's funny. He's—interesting, clever...."

Just then, Mickey reared up as a black-and-white shape came hurtling across the field toward him. "Ee-aww! Ee-aww!"

"And noisy!" Mrs. Brooks sighed. "And no, Ella, before you ask—I won't adopt Mickey!"

Ella's shoulders sagged.

"But it was worth a try," Mrs. Brooks said with a smile.

In any case, Ella had recognized the black-and-white creature racing through the long grass. "Bonnie!" she called.

The runaway dog barked and swerved
away from Mickey, then bounded
toward Ella.

"Sit!" Ella said sternly.

Bonnie obeyed.

"You're a bad girl," Ella said, wagging
her finger. "You've run away from home,
haven't you?"

Bonnie gazed up with her big, dark
eyes and an expression that said,

Please don't tell on me!

"And now I'm going to have to take you back." Ella tried not to smile at Bonnie's crestfallen look. "Heel!" she told her, setting off up the field.

Good as gold, Bonnie trotted along at Ella's side.

"I'm taking you back home," Ella told the runaway. "And I'm going to tell them to keep an eye on you." She talked quietly as they reached the road and turned right. "This is a busy road. You could've been run over. I bet it's Katie's fault," she grumbled. "She probably left the gate open. Sit, Bonnie. Wait for this car. Okay, now we can cross. Heel! Good girl—we're almost there!"

Chapter Ten

A Terrible Mistake

Ella took Bonnie up to the front door of the old, ivy-covered house and rang the doorbell. "Hello, is anyone home?"

There was no answer, so she walked around the side. "Hello?" she called again hopefully. She was anxious to drop off Bonnie and get back to Animal Magic.

It was Bonnie who decided what to do next. She trotted toward the back porch and pushed at the half-open door.

"Good girl," Ella muttered.

She followed Bonnie inside and went to
fill up a dish with fresh water as Bonnie
padded into the kitchen, looking for
Clyde.

Just as Ella finished, she spotted Katie
Platt through the open door, running up
the driveway.

"Have you seen Bonnie?" Katie gasped.
"We were taking the two dogs on a walk
by the river, but she ran away!"

Ella stared. Katie had obviously sprinted all the way home. Her fair hair was sticking to her forehead, and her face was pink. "Bonnie's here," she answered quietly. "I brought her back."

"I told Dad not to let her off the leash," Katie panted. "We were near the golf course, and she ran off to chase a ball. She wouldn't come back when we called."

Ella nodded. "I caught her in the field behind Mr. and Mrs. Brooks' house."

Katie pushed her hair back from her face. Then she ran to check on Bonnie. "Thank goodness!" she cried, peering around the kitchen door. "Here, Bonnie!"

Bonnie bounded out and jumped up at Katie, licking her face and leaving dirty paw marks on her T-shirt.

"Sit!" Katie pleaded. But as usual the excited dog ignored her.

"Do the arm movement at the same time," Ella said. "Like this. 'Sit!'"

This time, Bonnie obeyed Ella's command.

"You do it," Ella told Katie.

But Katie shook her head and headed out of the back porch. She began to trail back down the driveway.

"Hey, stop!" Ella called. She closed the door on Bonnie and ran after Katie. "It's easy. And Bonnie's a fast learner."

"I don't want to do it," Katie insisted. "If you're so clever, why don't you take them both—Bonnie and Clyde—and let them live with you at Animal Magic!"

The words stopped Ella in her tracks. Then she grew angry. "That's right—

send them to the rescue center. At least this time you're not just dumping them like you dumped Hamlet!"

Katie had reached the gates, but now she stopped, too. She turned to face Ella. "What are you talking about?" she asked slowly.

"I said, at least this time you're not dumping them in a garbage can and leaving them to die!"

"What? Who's Hamlet?" Katie insisted.

Ella felt as if she was about to burst, she was so mad. "You know who Hamlet is. And don't think I can't see why you want to send Bonnie and Clyde to Animal Magic. It's because you can't handle them, and you're jealous of Caleb and me because we can!"

"No, I'm not!" Katie's face had changed from flushed pink to deep red. She clenched her hands into fists.

Suddenly, Ella noticed the tears that had sprung to Katie's eyes. Her own anger fizzled out, and she stood puzzled in the middle of the driveway.

"Okay," Katie admitted. "I haven't been any good with Bonnie and Clyde. They jump up all the time and pull when they're on the leash. I never knew training them would be so hard. Mom and Dad haven't had any time to help me, and I felt silly when Mom asked you and Caleb. And besides, you wouldn't talk to me at school, and I didn't know why not...."

"Stop!" Ella begged. "Are you seriously saying that you don't know what you did wrong to make me not want to be your friend?"

Miserably, Katie shrugged. "I thought it was because I was new and Mom says I'm too shy."

"The reason I wouldn't be your friend isn't because you're new or shy—who cares about that! It's because of what you did to Hamlet," said Ella angrily.

"Who's Hamlet?" Katie cried again.

"Hamlet is the hamster you dumped in my grandpa's garbage can!" Ella said loud and clear. She stormed back to the porch and pointed to the empty cage. "That's his cage, as if you didn't know!"

Katie followed the direction of Ella's finger. "That's not Hamlet's!"

"Of course it is—stop pretending!"

"It's not," Katie insisted. "That cage belonged to Daisy."

It was Ella's turn to look shocked. "Who's Daisy?"

Katie blinked. "Daisy was my silver and gray hamster. She was only six months old. But she died just before we moved. I buried her in the yard."

Chapter Eleven
An Adoption Record

Ella left Katie's house in a daze and walked into her grandpa's garden center.

"Hello, Ella!" Grandpa came out from his office, took one look at her face, and guided her inside. "Tell me," he invited.

"Grandpa, I've done something awful!" She felt the tears well up and did nothing to try and stop them.

"Does this have anything to do with Katie Platt?" he asked gently.

Ella nodded. "I've made her really

upset, and it was totally my fault."

And she told him about the awful mistake she'd made, and how she'd shouted and made Katie cry. "It turns out it wasn't Katie after all," she sobbed. "It was someone else who dumped Hamlet!"

Her grandfather put his arm around her shoulder. "Ah, I see!"

"I feel so horrible, Grandpa. Katie had to bury Daisy in a grave at her old house, and she misses her so much!"

"Yes," he said. "You were a little bit hasty, Ella. That's the way you're made. Did you say you were sorry?"

Ella nodded. "But 'sorry' isn't enough."

"But in another way, you've helped Katie," her grandpa pointed out. "You and Caleb have spent a lot of time training her dogs. They're much better than they used to be."

Ella nodded. "And we could keep on doing that—if Katie wants us to. Or wants *me* to. Caleb could keep doing it, no problem—*he* hasn't done anything to upset her."

Grandpa let her sit for a while. "You just jumped to the wrong conclusion, Ella, and now you're trying to put it right. From now on things will be different between you and Katie."

"I hope…." Ella sniffed and stood up. "You're right!" she said more firmly. "Things *will* be different. Thanks, Grandpa. I have to go."

"Four!" Caleb reported when Ella returned to Animal Magic. "A man named Tony Watson came and offered Gus a home. He already has two Jack Russells, so Gus has gone to join them."

"Four," Ella sighed wearily. She went and sat behind the reception desk.

Caleb stared at her. "What's up?"

"Nothing." For a while Ella fidgeted and pretended to straighten the stacks of flyers. Then she jumped down from her stool and shot off into the small animals unit.

"Hi, Hamlet," she muttered when she reached his cage.

For a while Hamlet kept out of sight behind a mound of wood shavings. Then he crept out, and Ella spotted his sweet brown face. He peered at her with his button-bright eyes.

"So we'll never know who dumped you, Hamlet," Ella began in a gentle, serious voice. "And honestly, I wish I'd never tried to find out. I mean, what does it really matter as long as we find you a wonderful new home?"

Little Hamlet tipped his head to one side. *That's right—what does it matter?*

"Someone will love you," Ella promised, putting her face right up to the bars of his cage. "Sooner or later, we'll find you the perfect owner!"

"Where's Mom? I need to give her a message!" Ella had made up her mind and dashed back out into the reception area.

"What message?" Caleb asked.

"Here, let me write it down." Ella scribbled a note and pushed it toward him. "No time to explain. Just make sure Mom gets this and does what it asks. I'm in a hurry. I have to spring-clean Hamlet's cage!"

It was five o'clock—time for Animal Magic to close its doors—when Mrs. Platt arrived with Katie.

Mom was chatting with Caleb and

Joel in the reception area. "Ah, Julia,
I'm glad you got my message," she said
with a mysterious smile. "Ella's in the
small animals unit waiting for Katie."

Mrs. Platt whispered in Katie's ear
and ushered her inside.

Katie looked nervous. She glanced at
the two harlequin rabbits, and Lulu and
Lacy. Then she moved on down the row.

"Hi, Katie," Ella said quietly. She was
standing beside Hamlet's cage.

Katie relaxed when she saw Hamlet.
"Hi!" she replied, getting as close
to Hamlet as she could. "You're so
handsome."

"Would you like to hold him?" Ella
offered.

Shyly, Katie opened the cage and
lifted Hamlet out. "Soft and silky,"

she muttered. "He's beautiful!"

Little Hamlet twitched his nose and looked up at Katie.

"Mom thinks he's probably only about three months old," Ella said. "But he's really tame and nice to handle."

"Yes." Katie's face was all smiles.

"So I was wondering, since you already know how to take care of hamsters, and considering my mom called your mom to ask if it would be okay—I was wondering if you'd like to give Hamlet a home."

"She said yes!" Ella announced, carrying Hamlet's cage and leading Katie back to the reception area.

Joel was already filling out the form. "Hamlet," he wrote in the space requesting the adopted pet's first name. "Platt" he wrote in the space asking for the last name.

"What's Hamlet's favorite treat?" an excited Katie asked Ella.

"Apples, but not too much. And if he's sleeping, don't try to pick him up."

Katie nodded. "I used to whistle to Daisy and she'd come to the front of her cage. Do you think I can teach Hamlet to do that?"

"Definitely!" Ella couldn't tell who was the happiest—herself, Katie, or Hamlet. "Make that five!" She grinned at Caleb, who was taking Hamlet's name off the website. *Five adoptions in one day!*

"And you can come and see Hamlet whenever you like," Katie told Ella.

"Tomorrow?" Ella asked in a flash. She held the door open for Mrs. Platt to carry the cage out to the car. "What time?"

"I'll see you at school to arrange it," Katie promised, hurrying out to the car.

Five! Hugo, Buster, Frankie, Gus, and, best of all, Hamlet! Ella waved good-bye to Katie as her mom drove off.

And now her dad was crossing the yard toward the animal hospital with a person Ella recognized—a dark-haired woman—oh, yes, Jen Andrews!

"Meet our new assistant," Dad announced. "Jen's going to replace Joel."

"Welcome to Animal Magic!" Mom

smiled at Jen, standing in the doorway with Joel, Caleb, and Ella beside her.

"Yes, and good luck," Joel added. "You'll need it if you're going to work with this animal-crazy family!"

Jen nodded, then smiled as her eyes settled on Ella's happy face. "I have a good feeling about this place," she said. "I'm sure I'm going to be very happy here!"